tHE runaWay HuG

For Mum – NB

For Jen, Peter, Max, Adrian, Harriet and Sebastian – FB

Scholastic Canada Ltd.
604 King Street West, Toronto, Ontario M5V 1E1, Canada

Scholastic Inc.
557 Broadway, New York, NY 10012, USA

Scholastic Australia Pty Limited
PO Box 579, Gosford, NSW 2250, Australia

Scholastic New Zealand Limited
Private Bag 94407, Botany, Manukau 2163, New Zealand

Scholastic Children's Books
Euston House, 24 Eversholt Street, London NW1 1DB, UK

Illustrations created in pastel
Typset in Livory

Library and Archives Canada Cataloguing in Publication
Bland, Nick, 1973-
The runaway hug / Nick Bland ; illustrated by Freya Blackwood.
ISBN 978-1-4431-1369-4
I. Blackwood, Freya II. Title.

PZ7.B557Ru 2012   j823'.92   C2011-905975-4

First published by Scholastic Australia in 2011.
This edition published in Canada by Scholastic Canada Ltd. in 2012.
Text copyright © 2011 by Nick Bland.
Illustrations copyright © 2011 by Freya Blackwood.
All rights reserved.

6 5 4 3 2 1   Printed in China 53   12 13 14 15 16 17

tHE runaway HuG

NICK BLAND & FREYA BLACKWOOD

Scholastic Canada Ltd.
Toronto New York London Auckland Sydney
Mexico City New Delhi Hong Kong Buenos Aires

"Mommy," said Lucy. "Can I have a hug before I go to bed?"
"Oh dear," said Mommy. "I only have one left. It's my very last hug."
"Can I borrow it?" said Lucy. "I promise I'll give it back."

It was long and soft, and Lucy thought it was very nice.
"Thank you," said Lucy. "I'll bring it back as soon as I'm
finished with it."

And she dashed off to find Daddy.

"Daddy," said Lucy. "Would you like a hug? It's the very last one, so you have to promise to give it back."
"I promise," said Daddy, and Lucy gave him Mom's very last hug.
"Now can I have it back?" said Lucy.

Daddy picked her up and squeezed
her as tight as a knot.
The hug was stronger than before,
but just as nice.

So she ran off to find the twins.

"Boys," said Lucy, "would you like a hug?"

"Nooooo, yuck," said the boys.

"But it's the very last one," said Lucy, and before the boys could run away, she squeezed them both tightly.

"Now can I have it back?" said Lucy.
The boys grumbled, but they gave her the hug together.
It was twice as big as before, but just as nice.

So she skipped away to find Lily.

"Would you like a hug, Lily?" said Lucy.
Lily always wanted a hug.

She threw open her little arms and Lucy gave her a great big hug.
Before Lucy could ask for it back, Lily giggled and hugged her again.
It smelled like peanut butter, but it was just as nice as before.

So she raced off to find Annie.

Annie was very naughty, but Lucy loved her just the same.
"Would you like a hug, Annie?" she said.
Annie woofed, so Lucy leaned over and gave her a peanut-buttery hug.

But as soon as she let go, Annie turned around and ran straight out the door, taking Mommy's very last hug with her.

Lucy chased her down
the hall and up the stairs

and in and out of every room,
but Annie was just too fast.

Lucy felt terrible. She wanted to cry.

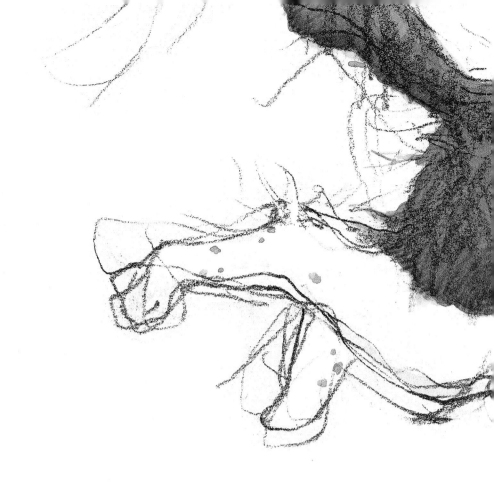

She was about to go tell Mommy she had lost her last hug
when Annie jumped out from nowhere. She landed right on
top of Lucy and licked her all over her face.
The hug was a lot more slobbery than before, but just as nice.

By the time Lucy got to her room, Mommy was waiting.
She climbed into bed and gave the last hug back
to Mommy. It was a little sleepier, but just as nice as
before, and Mommy was very glad to have it back.

"Can I have a kiss?" said Lucy.
"Of course you can," said Mommy.
"I have plenty of those."